The Witches' Supermarket

SUSAN MEDDAUGH

Houghton Mifflin Harcourt
Boston   New York

Library of Congress Cataloging-in-Publication data is on file.
ISBN: 978-0-395-57034-0 hardcover
ISBN: 978-0-395-70092-1 paperback
ISBN: 978-0-544-32358-2 with stickers

Printed in China
SCP 10 9 8 7 6 5 4
4500652284

"I just love Halloween!"
said Helen to her dog Martha.

"I'm sorry you don't like your costume,"
Helen said, "but witches have cats, not dogs.
Everybody knows that."

There was hardly anyone on the street when Helen and Martha set out to go trick-or-treating. One old woman hurried along ahead of them. She was short and round, and as she turned a corner, something fell from her bulging purple pocket.

Helen picked it up. "It's a coupon," she said. "Hey, lady!" But the woman didn't hear her. Helen took the coupon and ran after her.

The old woman moved along at a surprisingly fast pace. She ducked down an alley and was disappearing behind a door when Helen and Martha turned the corner. It was a very dark alley and Helen hesitated. Finally she said, "Come, Martha. We are not afraid!"

Helen stopped at the door. Signs read:

PRIVATE

KEEP OUT

MEMBERS ONLY

TRESPASSERS WILL BE SORRY

The biggest sign of all said:

NO DOGS ALLOWED

"Grrrrr," said Martha.

"I wonder what kind of a place this is," said Helen nervously. She knocked on the door. No one answered.

"Hello," she said in a small voice. Then she opened the door just a crack to peek inside.

"It's just a supermarket!" she announced.
"Come, Martha. That lady will be very happy
to get her coupon back."

Inside the store Helen noticed several cats. "It's no fair to allow cats and not dogs," she said to Martha. "It's lucky you have your costume on."

Still, Helen was a little worried, so she took a shopping cart and told Martha to hop in. "Remember," she said, "no barking!"

Apples with worms 79¢

Poison Apples

Don't forget the Beebleberries

Apples without worms 13¢

This Week's MYSTERY SPECIAL

Poison Mushrooms

Deadly Nightshade

Deadly Hemlock

Giant Black Henbane

Poison Ivy

Poison Sumac

Goatweed

Climbing Nightshade

OUR FRUIT IS NEVER FRESH. PUT SOME ON YOUR TABLE AND WATCH IT GROW

Helen looked for the woman in the purple coat. She didn't notice the unusual fruits and vegetables in the produce department.

Up and down the aisles she went.
There was a terrible stink in the dairy department.

ROTTEN EGGS, said a sign.

Martha was very
disappointed in the
pet food section.

"I'm glad Momma doesn't shop here," said Helen
as they came to the meat department.

Everyone is certainly ready for Halloween, thought Helen.

"I have never ever seen a supermarket like this,"
said Helen as she came to household products. There
was no soap for washing dishes, clothes, or floors.
There were no sponges, mops, or vacuum cleaner bags.
There were brooms, however. Lots and lots of brooms.

And standing there looking at the brooms was the woman in the purple coat.

The old woman carefully picked a broom from the large display. She studied it from every angle.

What is she doing? wondered Helen.

Helen suddenly wanted to go home.

"Let's get out of here," Helen whispered to Martha.
But as she turned to go, a large figure loomed above her.
"May I help you?" said the manager of the store.

"No, thank you," Helen stammered. "I was just going to pick up some . . . dog food."

"DOG FOOD!" shrieked the manager in a voice that could be heard three aisles away. "Did you say DOG FOOD?"

BROOMS – Every S

Deluxe
Brooms

Handle
with
CARE

Used
Broo

From up and down the aisles Helen could hear angry voices. "Dog food," they said. "Did she say dog food?"

"Witches don't have dogs," they said, and they began to chant:

"SHE'S NOT A WITCH. SHE'S NOT A WITCH. DON'T LET HER OUT THE DOOR! THE WITCHES' SUPERMARKET WON'T BE A SECRET ANYMORE!" Then from the shopping cart came a most un-catlike growl.

GRRRRRR

"A dog!" gasped the manager.
Cats, thought Martha.
Over, under, and around
the witches they ran.

The brooms went wild.

"Stop the brooms!" shouted the manager. But it was too late.
It was Halloween, and the brooms were ready to fly.
Helen grabbed on to a broom heading for the door.

"Stop that girl!" shouted the check-out witch. "Get that dog."

Helen and Martha made it through the alley.

   "There she is!" said the manager.

   "No, she's over there!" said a witch.

   "Where's the dog?" yelled another.

   But there were cats everywhere and the witch
costume was just too popular that year.

Later that night, Helen's mother said,
"I've got to run over to the supermarket to
pick up some dog food. Want to come?"
"Grrrrrrr," said Martha.